Alison's Fishing Birds

Roderick Haig-Brown
Foreword by Andrew Nikiforuk

Illustrations by
Sheryl McDougald
and Jim Rimmer

CAITLIN PRESS

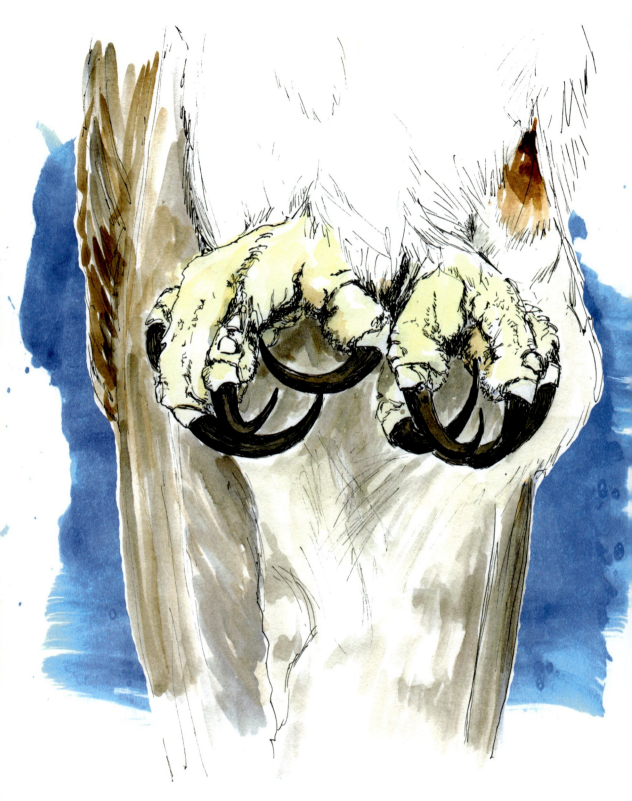

Osprey Talons

FOREWORD

Roderick Haig-Brown spent much of his life (1908-1976) observing fish and birds in the wild or challenging wrong-headed projects that threatened their homes. As one of Canada's great wilderness fathers, Haig-Brown wrote with a startling sense of urgency and timelessness. He actually believed that every Canadian should keep the waters and forests near their communities in wild healthy states because it would make them happier human beings.

As a rural author, Haig-Brown wrote with the urgency of Wallace Stegner and the moral authority of Wendell Berry. He listened to what the rivers and forests had to say about right-livelihood in Canada, and was never afraid to write about the wonder of existence. He believed in truth and accuracy and recognized there were limits to the human economic adventures. Much of his writing was philosophical — an occupation Canadians have about as much interest in as proctology. Haig-Brown was really never sure whether his work as conservationist ever did him or anyone else any good but defending clear waters that sustained fish or fowl always seemed like the most hopeful thing a person could ever do.

More importantly Haig-Brown understood that humans sprang from Nature and, despite all of our silly gadgets, remained a people of the Ice Age. He never thought of Nature as some sort of luxury, accessory or beautiful artifact ... because it is an inalienable part of us. A species can't spend 50,000 generations of its existence hunting and gathering and not have that activity leave a hefty impression on its soul. And that's why Haig-Brown liked watching mergansers paddle a river or herons scour the sky, because their presence helped him feel and think. Any engagement with wildlife — whether listening to the chatter of river otters, hunting grouse or watching a black bear denude an apple tree — restored human meaning and brought us back to the point of things: there is no end to wonder and joy when you care about a place.

Alison's Fishing Birds passes that joy onto another generation.
—Andrew Nikiforuk

PREFACE

In the late 1980s I began the job of editing my father's papers. These papers are all either in the University of British Columbia library or in his study at the house in Campbell River, and I started by spending several weeks reading. If I had found nothing of interest it would still have been a delightful task. Time spent in the quiet of a university library, in the garden in September sunshine or in front of the fireplace during October rain reading my father's manuscripts, galleys and letters could hardly be considered lost. As it was, I found enough material for several collections, much of it previously published in magazines. Rarely did I come across anything unpublished. My father was a serious writer who sold his first piece at sixteen and whose income during most of his life depended on selling what he wrote. But once in a while I found something that for some reason did not sell, was returned by his New York agent and gradually drifted to the bottom of the desk drawer. Of the rather short list of such pieces — in all my reading, really — *Alison's Fishing Birds* was my personal high point. I had never read it before (though possibly it was read to me) and I could not help being thoroughly charmed, both as an editor and a daughter.

I have not been able to find any specific date for the writing of *Alison's Fishing Birds*, but from various clues it seems to have been written in 1939 or '40, which may explain the lack of a sale. The times were not very good for book publishing, generally, let alone books for children. I would have been three or four years old and my sister Mary, two years younger. It is most likely that Alison is a composite of those two little girls who certainly did live "beside the river" in "the brown house with the pale blue trim." I also came across two or three shorter stories for younger children that were written about that time and, with *Alison*, are all the writing my father did for very young children. Perhaps this is because over the next few years his time was taken up with army service and because the fly-fishing books, *The Western Angler* and *A River Never Sleeps*, as well as *Return to the River*, were beginning to be successful.

I am not a great believer in coincidence, but sometimes I wonder a little. One afternoon a couple of days after I found *Alison*, I took a break from my fireside reading to walk a little now that the rain had let up. I walked down the lawn from the study and started up the river with no purpose other than a little fresh air. Before long I was "near the pasture fence, where there is a little sandy beach at the edge of the river, hidden by thick-growing willows." I like to think the dipper that just then was "perched on a rock ... not more than half a dozen steps away" was a descendant of Alison's dipper.

I often think of *Alison's Fishing Birds* as a tiny gem and I was delighted when, in 1980, Jim McIntosh and Jim Rimmer from Colophon Press published an exquisite, leather-bound collectors' edition of the story. I am equally delighted that Caitlin Press has now produced this beautifully illustrated trade edition, so it may be enjoyed, by children, parents, grandparents and educators everywhere.

Valerie Haig-Brown — 2017

ALISON'S FISHING BIRDS

It is rather well worth writing about all Alison's birds, for at least two reasons. First, because Alison's house beside the river, the brown house with the pale blue trim on the windows, is in just the right place for Alison to see a lot of birds. And secondly because Alison is a quick little girl who likes to watch birds as well as almost anything, so that she generally sees what the birds are really like and what they really do.

When Alison was a very little girl she used to see birds often enough — sometimes out of the window of her house; sometimes when she was outdoors and they flew over or perched in a tree or on a fence-post; and sometimes, when there was snow, they would be on the porch eating bread crumbs that she had put out for them. And at bedtime she used to make her father tell her stories about them and what they had been doing.

Alison's father generally wanted Alison to go to sleep instead of listening to stories all night, and pretty soon he would say to Alison, "But that little bird went to sleep long ago. Just as soon as it was beginning to get dark he looked up and said to himself,

'Time to go to sleep.' Then he flew and flew til he came to his favourite tree. And flew into the tree, found his favourite little branch, perched on it, and put his little head down and went sound asleep." He would say the last few words very quietly and slowly and generally Alison would feel sleepy and put her own little head down and go sound asleep.

But when she was a little older, Alison used to go out along the river or down to the slough or into the woods and quite often she found stories about the birds for herself. You couldn't call Alison a naturalist or a bird watcher or anything dull like that. She didn't sneak and peer and creep around looking for birds, but she liked to go up the river and she was quiet and her eyes were quick; so she saw quite a lot, and if she was in the mood and there was a bird of some sort hopping or perching near her she loved to watch it and see what it would do. Besides being fun it gave her new stories to tell her dolls when she put them to bed.

MERGANSER
DUCKLING

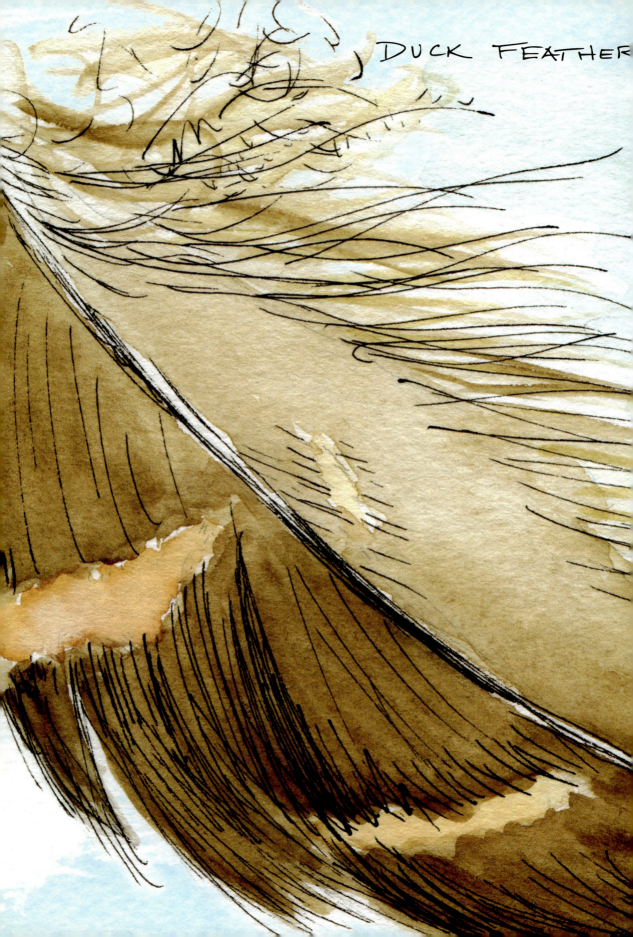

DUCK FEATHER

PACIFIC TREE FROG

SPOT PRAWN

BUMBLE BEE

WATER OUZEL

ONE

ALISON'S DIPPER

One of Alison's favourite birds, and one of the easiest to watch too, is the dipper — more proper people than Alison and her father sometimes call it the water-ouzel. The dipper Alison watches most often lives along the river between her house and the Sandy Pool. She has seen it hundreds of times — on the rocks of the dam that shelters the water-wheel down at her house, on the old slippery logs and sandy beaches of the Sandy Pool, anywhere and everywhere along the banks of the river. The dipper is not a very big bird — larger than a sparrow but much smaller than a robin, very round and important and merry. His colours are sober, almost dull, unless you look at them very closely: a dark-grey back that seems bluish sometimes when the light is on it, a head still dark-grey but with more of brown in it than the back, a breast scarcely lighter than the rest of him, and pale slender olive-green legs. But Alison loved him for his brisk light movements, his flirting stubby tail and his friendliness.

Though she saw the dippers often, Alison always remembers best of all one particular spring day, and it was the story of that she always told her dolls. It was a warm, lazy day, almost as warm and lazy as the real summer days, and Alison had gone only a little way up the river when she felt she would like to lie down and just think. So she went to a secret place she had near the pasture fence, where there is a little sandy beach at the edge of the river, hidden by thick-growing willows and marked off by a tall alder on the downstream side and an old twisted crabapple on the upstream side. The sand was dry and clean so she lay down in it, looking out across the white leaping water of the wide rapid where the river breaks from the Sandy Pool. Almost at once there was a quick dark little streak of grey from downstream and the dipper was perched on a rock in front of Alison, not more than half a dozen steps away from her.

Alison had been feeling almost a little drowsy, but now her eyes opened wide and she kept very, very still. The dipper did not seem to have noticed her and stood on the rock for a few moments, quite still except that his bright little eyes twinkled and blinked. Then, just as suddenly as he had arrived, he flew from the rock to the sand in front of Alison and began to strut and run along the edge of the water. Soon he was wading into the water, so that his legs were quite hidden and the tiny waves lapped his breast feathers. Then Alison could only see his head. Then that disappeared too and he had walked right under the water.

Alison got up very quietly and stood leaning against the crabapple tree. She could see the dipper walking along the bottom of the river, still with his little jerky movements, turning his head this way and that. He reached forward sharply and seemed to catch something in his beak, then bobbed up to the surface of the water. For a moment he sat there like a little grey duck, shaking the water from his dumpy tail. Then he flew with his quick little flight to another rock and perched on that.

Alison watched him with all her attention, making up the story to tell her dolls. He was never still. Standing on the rock, without moving his feet, he bobbed his little round body up and down, bob, bob, bob. And with each bob there was a little flash of white as his eyelids came up to cover his eye in a blink. Bob, bob, bob, blink, blink, blink; bob-blink, bob-blink, bob-blink. Alison said it over to herself very quietly, so that he would not hear her.

Suddenly, with a quick skittering movement, he was off the rock and swimming in the water again. The bobbing seemed to go on as he swam, poking his head forward, searching under the water with his shiny black eyes. Then, with a great big bob and a flick of his tail, he dived right under the water. This time Alison could see him swimming hard, with his grey wings and his little legs working for all they were worth. And in front of him, swimming its hardest, too, was a little fish. But the dipper swam faster and caught the little fish, then came to the surface so fast that he fairly popped out into the air and bounced a little as he sat there. He swam along for a few strokes with the little fish shining and wriggling in his beak, then flew (flitter-fly, flitter-fly said Alison to herself, and that was really very much how he did fly) to perch on yet another rock.

On the rock he went bob, bob, bob, and blink, blink, blink. Then he put his little head back and swallowed the little fish. When that was over he went on bobbing and blinking as though nothing at all had happened. Alison was rather worried. She had never thought of the little dippers eating fish before, and she had often heard her father and other men talking about birds that ate fish; her father didn't seem to mind very much, but most of the other men thought that they ought to shoot all the birds that ate fish. Alison decided to say something to the dipper. "That's pretty bad of you, you know," she said. "You shouldn't catch little fish and eat them like that."

DIPPER

The dipper didn't stop his bobbing and blinking at all, but he put his little head on one side and looked up at Alison. "Guess I've got to live, haven't I?" he asked. "And guess I've got to eat to live." "Yes," Alison said. "But not little fish. Or their eggs. You can catch caddis grubs and beetles and things like that — I know, because I've seen you."

The dipper bobbed several times. "Easier to get the fish this time of year. There's plenty of 'em anyhow — meant for me, just this way. I take a lot of little fish and you have me. The merganser takes a lot of little fish and you have him. And you have enough little fish left over to make some big fish. Isn't it better to have a lot of different things instead of a lot of the same things?"

Alison didn't know quite what to say to that, but she tried anyhow. "Well, I'm sure it's not right. I've heard them say so lots of times. And I'm afraid they might come and shoot you if you go on doing it."

The dipper didn't seem to think so. "Hardly," he said. "I'm too small. Anyway, it's salmon they want. And I'm like the merganser and the heron; I catch more bullheads than I do trout and salmon and the bullheads eat trout and salmon, so I help more than I hinder. You want to learn that sort of thing you know. We all fit in pretty neatly and help to keep things going smoothly."

The dipper skittered off the rock again, swam a few jerky little strokes, bobbed under the water, bobbed up again, and then flew. This time he went on up the river, close to the bank and very fast. Alison watched him and could see him turn off sharply to follow up the little creek that joined the river halfway up the Sandy Pool. She wondered how she could finish the story for her dolls. It was springtime and she knew the female dipper would be sitting on her white eggs in the round mossy nest with the entrance through a hole at the side. She even knew where the nest was on a ledge of rock right under the tumbling falls of the little creek, so that the birds had to fly right through the falling water to reach it. But would the male sleep perched on the rock beside the nest — he never seemed to mind about the water — or would he go well away somewhere and find a comfortable branch in a willow bush? Alison was still wondering when she got home.

Kingfisher

Taxidermy:
Beaty Biodiversity
Research Centre

TWO

THE KINGFISHER

Another bird that Alison saw very often beside the river was the belted kingfisher — she sometimes thought they might almost as well have named him the laughing kingfisher or the crested kingfisher, because he laughed so loud and his crest was so large and ragged and splendidly handsome. For that matter he was handsome all over, his slate-blue back, speckled with the white-tipped feathers of his folded wings, his white throat and lower breast, his long sharp beak and bright eye with the white spot just in front of it, were handsome as handsome could be. And his belt, more like a lord-mayor's chain really, set over his shoulders and curving down to a point on his chest, could only make the whole effect just a little more splendid.

Very often when Alison saw him he was just flying on his way up or downstream. Sometimes with a sudden loud rattle of laughter he would swoop sharply upwards in his flight and perch abruptly on the branch of a tree or on the very top of a dead

15

snag leaning out over the water. Alison soon got to know some of his favourite perching places and she saw him come back to them again and again. They were always high places, chosen to give him a clear view into the river and down to the very rocks on the bottom.

Alison found her kingfisher story in the same spring as she found her dipper story. She was walking up the river one day when the kingfisher came from behind her and turned suddenly from his swift swooping flight to perch on the dead top of a cedar tree that leaned out over the water. He sat very still, not looking at Alison, not even looking down into the water, but with his eyes gazing ahead, straight up the river. His big strong beak was thrust forward so that his shoulders seemed a little hunched and his slender perching feet and claws held to the wood of the tree. Alison had moved forward a little and she could see that his lower breast was pure white; the female kingfisher always has a reddish colour in her breast feathers, so she knew this one was a male.

Suddenly there was a flash of slate-blue and white from upstream and another kingfisher swooped up towards the cedar top. Alison's kingfisher met him in mid-air, a few feet above the tree, and for a moment or two there was a confused hovering and beating of wings and terrible noise of harsh scolding. Then the second kingfisher turned and began to fly up and away, with Alison's kingfisher close behind him, still scolding and chattering. They went for a short distance like this, then Alison's kingfisher turned sharply away and came swooping back to his perch; the other swung off into the woods and was soon lost among the trees.

For a few moments Alison's kingfisher was very busy on his perch ducking his beak down into his breast feathers and under his wing. Alison saw one or two downy little feathers float away from him, as though he had been pulling them out of himself — which he had. She wondered if she ought to say anything, in case he was

16

still angry about the other kingfisher. But finally she decided she might as well. "I think you've lost one or two feathers," she said.

"Naturally enough," he answered, a little harshly. "Got to keep things in shape if you want to fly well. Got to get rid of the old ones that aren't good anymore. Busy time of year, too, even without poachers around."

"Aren't there enough fish for both of you?" Alison asked. She remembered what the dipper had said about catching fish and anyway there wouldn't be much point in telling a bird called kingfisher that maybe he'd better not catch fish.

"We don't do things that way," the kingfisher said. "I always fish the same piece of river. Surely he can stick to his own place. And in the spring too, when there's a family to feed."

Suddenly he slipped from his perch and swooped out over the water. For a moment he hung in the air, quite still except that his wings were beating very fast. Then he dropped like a stone, head first in the water. Alison saw him come up again out of the splash and fly back to his perch. A little silvery fish was wriggling in his long black beak. He knocked the little fish two or three times against the tree, then swallowed it.

Almost at once he dived again, this time straight from his perch, and in a moment he was back again with another fish, shaking the water from his wings with a quick movement of his body. He swallowed that fish and six more that he caught one after another. He seemed to be a very good fisherman and the old cedar snag seemed to be a very good place to fish from.

"Aren't you eating an awful lot?" Alison asked him. "If you go on like that all day you won't be able to fly."

"Listen," said the kingfisher, looking down at her fiercely. "You know where the old gravel pit is about half a mile up the road from the bridge?"

"Yes," Alison told him. "That's where your nest is, in a hole in the bank. I've seen you go in there."

"Well there's a bunch of youngsters in that nest and they've got to eat something, haven't they?"

"Yes," Alison said.

"Well that's what I'm doing. Getting food for them."

Alison looked puzzled. "But what good is it going to do if you eat all the fish yourself?"

"I can spit 'em up again, can't I?" said the kingfisher. And while Alison was still thinking about that he slipped from his perch again and went off downstream with a loud rattle of laughter to take the fish back to his nest.

COASTAL
GUM
PLANT

WESTERN
RED-BACKED
SALAMANDER

20

STARRY FLOUNDER

DRAGONFLY

CLAM SHELL

SHORE CRAB
CLAW

SECONDARY WING FEATHER

THREE

THE HERON

Perhaps the most skilful of all the fishing birds that lived near Alison's house were the herons. Alison saw them almost every evening as they flew up the river on slow, wide wings from a day of feeding along the beaches or on the flats at the mouth of the river. She liked them because they were so slow and calm and dignified, and because they were so big. Standing on their long legs and with their long necks held straight up, they were taller than Alison herself, and she was quite a tall little girl for her age. The spread of their wings was as great as the height of Alison's father and he was a tall man.

One day Alison was walking down the trail toward the mouth of the river, to go and play with another little girl who was a friend of hers. She stopped at one place where she could walk out along a pile of rocks, because sometimes she had been able to look into the water and see little fish from there. Just as she started to go out on the rocks she saw a great shadow slipping over the ground, so she

COHO FINGERLING

SEAGULL FEATHER

GREAT BLUE HERON

stopped at once and stood very still, looking up at the big heron who had made the shadow. He did not see her at all, because she was still under the trees, and he pitched down gracefully at the edge of the water.

He was so close that Alison could even see the black pupil of his eye. He was a very splendid bird, much more splendid than she expected because she had always seen herons in the distance before and they looked just grey. This heron — Alison called him old Walk-up-the-Creek to herself, because some people call all herons that and somehow the name seemed to fit this one — old Walk-up-the-Creek had a grey back all right, but he had much more than that. His long bill, as strong and sharp as a sword, was yellow. His head was white and two long dark plumes curved back from it. His throat and breast were white, but speckled handsomely with light brown. There were more plumes on his throat and on his back, and altogether he seemed a magnificent bird.

Alison had time to see all this because he stood quietly at the edge of the water, on one leg with the other drawn up under him, for several minutes. Then he began to walk, very slowly and smoothly, out into the water. It was quite shallow and soon he stopped again and stood quite still, on both feet this time. His neck was drawn in so that his head was hunched between his shoulders; but his great strong beak was pointing down a little and Alison could see that he was looking hard down into the water.

He stood so long like that that one of Alison's feet went to sleep and she wanted to scratch her nose and wanted to pull her dress down a little on her shoulder, where it was uncomfortable. But she didn't move because she knew old Walk-up-the-Creek was going to catch a fish and she wanted to see him do it. And all at once he did it, so quickly that Alison hardly saw how, though she was watching all the time. His head seemed to jump forward, his long beak went down into the water and out again in the tiniest part of a second and there was the fish, held so firmly that it hardly wriggled at all.

For nearly a minute old Walk-up-the-Creek didn't seem to pay any attention to the fish in his beak; he simply stood there looking just as he had before he caught it. Then he lifted his beak, put his head back and swallowed the little fish, and Alison could see a ripple as it slid all the way down his long neck.

As soon as the little fish was out of the way old Walk-up-the-Creek began fishing again. This time he held his head forward a little more and his body was tilted forward too. And instead of standing quite still he walked forward through the water, but so slowly that it hardly seemed like walking, though Alison couldn't think what else to call it. He lifted first one foot, then the other, so slowly and gently that it really seemed as though he wasn't moving at all. And quite suddenly his beak darted down again and Alison saw he had caught another fish.

This time he swallowed it more quickly and, just as he was starting to fish again, Alison's nose tickled so much that she sneezed. Old Walk-up-the-Creek didn't wait to see that it was only a little girl. He flapped his great wings, squawked angrily and flew heavily away. Alison watched the little ripples on the water where he had been standing and felt sorry she had frightened him so much. But she had to go on and play with her friend and couldn't wait for him to come back.

That evening just before dark, when Alison was back at her own house again, she saw a heron flying up the river towards the big trees where they always roost. He was a fine big heron and Alison watched him carefully, wondering if he was old Walk-up-the-Creek. His broad dark wings moved very slowly; his long beak was pointing sharply straight in front of him, his head was hunched back between his shoulders; his thin legs were stiffly together, held straight out behind him.

HERON
FEATHERS

COHO SALMON

Alison couldn't see his plumes or the white of his head and breast; he was just grey and big against the sky. But as he flew past her he croaked loudly, just once. The herons don't generally croak when they are flying up past the house in the evenings, so Alison knew it must be old Walk-up-the-Creek, and he must have remembered her.

BLADDER WRACK
SEAWEED

31

MERGANSER
DUCKLING

FOUR

THE MERGANSERS

The fishing birds that Alison saw most often and most easily in her river were the American mergansers. There were always some playing and splashing and swimming along the rapid that ran past her house. She saw them whenever she went to the Sandy Pool. And there were more of them farther up the river, among the Islands, and farther down the river on the tide flats and in the slough.

For most of the year Alison saw only females and young birds. They were handsome enough, with their grey backs, their red-brown heads and their ragged crests, sitting easily on the water and swimming with strong strokes of their pale feet. But in the spring the male birds came and these were so handsome that Alison held her breath for a moment whenever she saw one.

One winter, when Alison was seven or eight years old, she made friends with an old female merganser who spent a lot of time in the still water behind the little wing-dam that Alison's father had built out into the river near the house. Every afternoon, as soon as she got back from school, Alison used to go very quietly down to the river and nearly always the merganser was there. At first she used to fly off whenever Alison came, but soon she got to know that Alison would not hurt her. Then she just went on with her business, swimming all the time out towards the swifter water of the rapids, and at last drifting down and away with it, but not frightened at all.

Sometimes the merganser would keep swimming so close to the bank of the river that Alison could see the short, jagged teeth in her orange bill. Alison's father told her that the merganser was a female, so Alison called her Mrs. Sawbill. And Alison's father had told her that when spring came Mrs. Sawbill might just possibly have a nest down there somewhere near the wing-dam and raise a family of little Sawbills.

This seemed very exciting to Alison and as spring came she was more and more careful to go down to the river every day and as many times a day as she could. And at last one day towards the middle of March she went down there and found two mergansers, Mrs. Sawbill and a great big handsome male. The male flew away at once and Mrs. Sawbill edged out in the current far more quickly than usual; and soon as she had drifted down a little way she flew off after him.

The next day Alison went down to the river more quietly and carefully and found them both there again. This time the male (Alison called him Mr. Sawbill already) was less nervous or else he didn't see Alison at all, because both of them stayed there behind the dam and went on with what they were doing. At first they didn't seem to pay much attention to each other, but soon Alison felt that Mr. Sawbill was swimming very proudly and carefully, trying to get Mrs. Sawbill to look at him and see what a fine fellow he was. As a matter of fact, Alison decided, he really was a fine-looking fellow. He was bigger and heavier than Mrs. Sawbill and

his head, instead of being red-brown, was a glossy dark green, so
dark that it was almost black. His back and wings were mostly
black and white and his breast was the loveliest, smoothest pale
creamy pink that Alison had ever seen.

After a little while Mr. Sawbill swam a circle round Mrs.
Sawbill. Then he lifted himself up from the water and flapped
his wings several times, showing off the beautiful plumage of his
breast. Then he kicked hard with one foot and splashed water high
in the air; Alison could see the beautiful bright orange colour of
his foot as it came out of the water, but Mrs. Sawbill still didn't
seem to be paying much attention. In a little while she edged out
into the swift water and dived under so that Alison could not see
her anymore. Mr. Sawbill followed, still swimming on top of the
water, and lifting his head high to look for her. She came up, far
downstream, and he flew towards her across the water. Before he
could reach her she was flying too and they both flew upstream,
beyond the Sandy Pool.

Alison saw them together again many times. Mr. Sawbill grew
more and more vigorous and acrobatic in the water, swimming and
diving and splashing and flapping his wings and showing himself
off in every possible way. Sometimes Mrs. Sawbill joined him in
all this, but generally she just swam about her business in a very
dignified way and refused to be greatly impressed.

Towards the end of April, Alison sometimes found Mr. Sawbill
alone, and once or twice, as she watched, Mrs. Sawbill came from
somewhere close by and joined him. Alison told her father about
this and he said that Mrs. Sawbill must have a nest somewhere.
A few days after that Alison and her father went to look for the
nest. Alison's father walked ahead of her, keeping along the edge
of the river and looking carefully up under the dry bank that is
only covered in floodtime. Soon he stopped and beckoned Alison
to come up to him. She came along on tiptoe, trying not to breathe

35

COMMON MERGANSER

MERGUS MERGANSER

too hard and looking at the bank where he was pointing. At first she could only see a tangle of many tree roots, then suddenly she could see Mrs. Sawbill's grey back tucked away amongst them and her red head, very still, held forward and low down. Alison and her father crept away very quietly.

Several days later, when Alison came back from school, her father said: "Mrs. Sawbill's off her nest. I saw her go up towards the Sandy Pool. We can go down and look at her eggs now if you are quick." So they went down along the river to where they had seen Mrs. Sawbill, and while her father kept watch to see if Mrs. Sawbill was coming back Alison crept up to the nest and looked in. She saw eleven eggs, a little larger than chicken eggs and a pale fawn colour. They were all neatly packed together in a hollow among the roots and Alison could see that Mrs. Sawbill had made a soft place for them with grass and moss and some of her own downy feathers. It was very exciting to be looking at the nest and the eggs looked so fresh and clean and Alison could almost feel that they were warm. But she was afraid that Mrs. Sawbill would come back and find her there and decide to leave them, so she and her father went away as quickly as they could.

Alison only saw Mrs. Sawbill once again after that and she was careful not to go near the nest again because she wanted Mrs. Sawbill to hatch out the eggs and bring up the little Sawbills close to her house.

Early in June Alison saw Mrs. Sawbill's family out on the water for the first time. She was careful not to go too close, but she could see that the little ducklings were round and fluffy and quite often she saw two or three of them riding on Mrs. Sawbill's back. They grew fast and soon began to look a lot like Mrs. Sawbill herself, only smaller. Generally they followed along behind their mother, swimming very smoothly and sedately, but sometimes they played hard and splashed water all over the place.

Mrs. Sawbill took them up in the river almost to the Sandy Pool and down the river almost to the bridge, but very seldom farther than that in either direction and Alison could nearly always see them when she went down to the river. Once or twice Alison was able to watch them from quite close because they came in and fished and dived and played right behind the dam. As they grew older they became busier and more active all the time.

The very last time Alison saw them all together was just before the spawning salmon began to die in the fall. She went down to the river one day to look for them and at first she couldn't see them at all. Then she noticed a lot of splashing in the shallow water down near the bridge. Among the splashes she could just see Mrs. Sawbill and all her little Sawbills.

In a little while they stopped splashing and began to work up the river. Mrs. Sawbill was swimming first, putting her head down under the water from time to time to look for fish. Suddenly she saw some and began to flap over the water at a great speed, half flying, half swimming. Behind came all the little Sawbills, half flying, half swimming too, and making a great splashing and noise. Then they began to dive after the fish, popping under water one after another until they were all out of sight. Then they began to pop up again, one after another and so suddenly that they seemed to bounce; it was very funny and Alison wanted to laugh out loud, but they were getting close now and she was afraid of frightening them.

After they had swallowed the little fish they had caught they came on up the river again. And just below the smooth water that lies in behind the dam they found some more little fish and went through all the flapping and diving again. When that was over they did what Alison always remembered afterwards. They all came swimming up through the still water behind the dam, Mrs. Sawbill leading and all the others, just like her now and almost as big, strung out behind her. They swam very proudly and sedately right past Alison as though they were on a parade. When they came to the dam they swam out past the end of it and began to fly. They flew together all the way up the rapid to the Sandy Pool, then round the bend and out of sight. And that was the last Alison saw of them because soon afterward the salmon began to die and there were so many mergansers on the river that she couldn't tell which was which. But Alison says she supposes they are all full-grown now and have families on their own.

FIVE

THE OSPREY

Though the osprey had his nest somewhere up among the big trees above the Sandy Pool he did not fish much in the river and generally when Alison saw him he was out over the sea near the mouth of the river. Alison liked him because he was bolder and swifter than the other fishing birds. Even when perched in one of the tall trees near her house, as he did sometimes on his way down the river, he seemed fierce and splendid and free. Alison's father said this was because he is a hawk and nearly all hawks are bold fierce birds.

The osprey was too bold and free for Alison ever to feel that she was friendly with him, as she was with the dipper and mergansers and some of the other birds. But whenever she saw him she felt somehow glad and happy and she couldn't help hoping that he would have good fishing.

She remembered best of all one summer day when she watched him fishing in the sea, just at the mouth of her river. She was out in a boat with her father and it was a fine summer day. The wind ruffled her hair and stirred the blue water into little white wavelets — a wind from the northwest that meant the weather would keep fine for a long time. Alison saw the osprey when he was still over the land, flying high above the trees towards the sea. Her father told her to watch him because he was sure to be fishing — it was the time of year when there would be young ospreys in the huge nest above the Sandy Pool, and young ospreys need lots of fish.

Alison watched the osprey coming swiftly towards her. He was a fine big bird, with a pure white front and a dark brown back. The underside of his wings was a mottled, paler brown. His neat white head had a crest of dark feathers and his beak was sharp and curved. He passed so close to the boat that she could see all this very clearly, and she watched the strong easy beat of his big wings as he flew down the channel with the wind behind him.

At first it seemed that he was going right away and Alison was afraid that she would not see him fishing after all. But when he had travelled down for a mile or so he swung in a great circle, mounting higher in the air, and began to fly back against the wind. He did not fly straight back, but swung back and forth across the channel as he worked up into the wind. Alison's father said that this was because he wanted to hunt over as much water as possible.

While the osprey was still working up the channel towards them Alison's father pointed towards the shore. "Look in the old fir tree," he said to Alison. Alison looked and she saw a great bald eagle sitting in one of the highest branches of the tree. She had seen the bald eagles often as they circled in the air above her house and she loved them for their great black wings and bodies and the splendid whiteness of their bold heads and broad tails against the sky. "He's watching the osprey," her father said. "But why?" Alison wanted to know. "What will he do?"

"You'll see in a minute," her father told her. "Look at the osprey now."

The osprey had stopped in his flight up the channel and was hovering over one spot, his wings beating the air to hold him in place. Suddenly he dropped, not straight down as the land hawks do, but in a swift spiral. When he was still a little way above the water he checked himself, hovered again, then dropped again. This time he hit the water with a great splash and for a second Alison could see nothing of him except perhaps the dark tip of one wing. Then he came up and tried to fly away from the water. His wings drove and drove against the air and splashed the water, but he did not move at all. He rested for a moment with his broad wings spread on the little waves, then tried again. But still he could not lift the fish he had seized in his claws. Once Alison could see the whole of his long legs and just the back of the fish, but that was his greatest effort. He sank back on the water, rested for a moment, then flew off without the fish. When he had gone only a few yards he stopped in mid-air and, with a quick movement of his wings and body, shook a shower of water from his feathers.

He did not seem angry or discouraged at the loss of his fish but worked on up the channel, still hunting. He stopped again, hovering, and dropped again, his long legs stretched out to their fullest length and his wings straight behind him in the air. He hit the water and came up almost at once. For a moment, he struggled, then he was free, in the air again, with a young salmon held firmly in his claws. "Now watch the eagle," said Alison's father quickly.

Alison looked towards the fir tree. The eagle had slipped away from it and was coming towards them, faster and faster on lazy wings that hardly seemed to move. The osprey had shaken the water from his feathers and was already in the air. He had seen the eagle and Alison felt that he was trying as hard as he could to get away. But the weight of the fish held him back. The eagle was very close and very big, flying straight towards the osprey. Alison thought they were bound to collide, but at the last moment the osprey seemed to slip away, down and to one side. And the eagle, his wings beating fast, his clawed feet stretched forwards, his white tail spread to its widest fan, swung sharply upwards.

The osprey had turned down with the wind and was flying his hardest. But the eagle was after him in a second and this time, as the osprey swung again to get away, he dropped his fish. It tumbled down towards the water, shining in the sun. After it came the eagle, faster and faster, and before it touched the water he had caught it in his claws. Alison watched him as he flew slowly off with it.

The osprey seemed to know that the eagle was too big and strong for him. He began to hunt again at once, working up the channel towards Alison and her father in the boat. He came closer and closer and, when he was almost opposite them, he hovered again and dropped again. Alison could hear the loud hiss of the air through his wings and could see the sharp claws at the end of his pale blue legs. Each drop of water from his splash sparkled in the sunshine and almost at once he was up again, trying to get away from the water with another small salmon in his claws.

But the wind was stronger that it had been and though he struggled to rise against it he could make little headway. When he was only a few feet above the water he gave up and dropped back. For nearly a minute he lay with his wings spread out, resting, then he tried again. This time he managed to fly a little higher, but he still could not make much headway against the wind, and Alison knew that he had to fly nearly a mile straight against it to reach his nest.

She turned to her father. "Couldn't we do anything to help him?" she asked.

Her father shook his head. "I'm afraid not," he said. "But watch him. I think he'll help himself in a minute."

The osprey was still above the water, flying up but hardly forwards at all. The strong wind against the flat side of the fish held him back. Then Alison saw him move his feet. He moved them so that he was holding the fish with its head pointing straight into the wind, and at once he began to make headway. Alison watched him as he flew off towards his nest and until he was only a tiny speck in the distance.

"Oh," she said at last. "I do hope he gets home with that one."

OSPREY SKULL

Caitlin Press Inc.
8100 Alderwood Road, Halfmoon Bay, BC V0N 1Y1
www.caitlin-press.com

Text design by Vici Johnstone
Cover design by Sheryl McDougald
Illustrations by Sheryl McDougald and Jim Rimmer, courtesy the Jim Rimmer Estate.
Sketch photo reference: Carl Olsen carl-olsen.pixels.com
Taxidermy reference: the Beaty Biodiversity Research Centre www.biodiversity.ubc.ca/
Assistant Curator of Birds Ildiko Szabo and Curatorial assistant of mammals, reptiles, and amphibians Chris Stinson

Printed in Canada

Caitlin Press Inc. acknowledges financial support from the Government of Canada and the Canada Council for the Arts, and the Province of British Columbia through the British Columbia Arts Council and the Book Publisher's Tax Credit.

Library and Archives Canada Cataloguing in Publication

Haig-Brown, Roderick L., 1908-1976, author
        Alison's fishing birds / written by Roderick L. Haig-Brown
: illustrated by Sheryl McDougald.

ISBN 978-1-987915-19-8 (hardcover)

        1. Birds—Juvenile literature. I. McDougald, Sheryl, 1957-,
illustrator II. Title.

QL795.B57H35 2017   j598   C2016-907721-7